Styra works at the Blue Station and has been programming since she was able to reach a keyboard. When she became an adult, she went from writing the simple scenarios and backgrounds to guiding tangled clients through the environments they had selected. Lately, she has been going in to pry out the difficult cases and making sure that everyone plays by the rules. Her boss calls her in on her day off and sends her in after an imperial captain. Somehow, he has gotten stuck in one of their fairy tale environments.

She headed in to find the missing client, and the computer had locked him in the role of the sleeping beauty. The criteria were clear. A kiss was necessary to wake him, and the protocols were set.

Once he was awake, she was ready to get him out of the scenario, but the computer was still locked.

Yr-el wasn't counting on his distaste for the virtual princess, but his drake had wanted to play in the scenario. When he wakes in the arms of a woman with moonlight for skin, he begins to understand why he was steered to this station at this time. All he had to do was get her to release the drake the same way she had released him, and he could begin a courtship.

Not Compatible
Copyright © 2020 by Viola Grace
ISBN: 978-1-989892-30-5

©Cover art by Angela Waters

Published by Viola Grace

Look for me online at violagrace.com. Available at eBook sellers.

Not Compatible
Stand-Alone Tales Book 11

By

Viola Grace

Chapter One

Styra grunted as she did another sit-up in the station gym. There were a few crewmen and women from some of the resupplying freighters working out. Still, most had facilities on their ships, so the gym was a luxury for the people who worked at the station.

Her com started pinging, and she groaned, sat up, and answered it. "Yeah?"

"Styra, please tell me you are near the center."

"I am, but today is my day off, sir." She wrapped a towel around her neck and started toward her locker to get her passes for travel in the Blue Station.

"What will it take you to come in?"

"Double time and a full-day spa pass." She grinned and waited for him to negotiate her down.

"Done. How soon can you be here?"

She was stunned. He never gave up that easily. There must be a disaster looming.

"I will be there in five. I am assuming an emergency retrieval is in order?" She grabbed her bag and fished out her passes. She waved at the attendant and headed out, tossing the towel into the hamper as she sprinted into the monstrous station that she called home.

"You presume correctly. Come to me directly when you arrive."

"Yes, sir. ETA three minutes." She hung up and continued her jog through the station toward the entertainment center.

In the four years she had worked for Mr. Blue, she had never gotten him to agree to her terms on the first offering.

There must be a VIP trapped in a scenario.

She scanned through security and headed up to Mr. Blue's office. She knocked when she was outside the executive suite, and he muttered, "Come in, Styra. We have a situation."

Mr. Blue was agitated. He was letting his human-seeming mask slip. His skin was bright blue, and his eyes were reptilian gold.

"Show me the file." She picked up the tablet and checked the file he sent her. She flicked through it and paused. "He's a drake hybrid?"

Mr. Blue grimaced. "Yes. He should be fine. There is no reason for him to have had an issue. We have two hours to straighten it out and get him free of the system."

"Why the time crunch?"

"Because he came in with some guards from the Ackerwol Imperium, and they want to leave with him."

She groaned. "Oh. Joy. Right. Okay, I am just going to finish scanning his file." She caught a few points of concern. Military service, high-stress position, and all of the accumulated experiences of three or four decades."

"Do you think you can sync to him?"

"I haven't run into anyone I couldn't sync to yet. I will take pod six."

"Great. Change and lock in. Time is literally money." Mr. Blue inclined his head.

He was resuming his human appearance, and she headed to the change room and sonic shower. She had prep to do and sweat to remove. She didn't need a rash on top of her other issues.

Styra smoothed the sensor suit on over her body and made sure that all of the pads and feedback material was in the right place for a proper drop into the scenario.

Her hair was pinned up, but the wrap around her face and ears would be the means by which her face was projected into the scenario.

She settled in her pod, put in the connection monofilament into the nearly invisible port that she had installed, and linked the pod to the captain's scenario. She was going to fall and land in the world he had chosen.

She dropped and landed on the ground, looking around at the surprising fairy tale landscape. Men usually chose this scenario when they had a companion who had either been with them or paid for. She was currently wearing the adventurer clothing that she preferred in this game. She liked to be able to move and climb with ease.

The display built into her headgear showed her that the client was two kilometers away, right under that swirling pile of drakes. *What fun.*

Styra set out at a jog and kept an eye out for any of the drakes changing direction. When she arrived near the coordinates, she saw the bramble wall and sighed, pulling out her blade. She touched it with the blade, and the brambles and thorns rustled angrily. She spoke softly, "I just want to help him. Please, let me through."

The brambles and thorns pulled apart and gave her ten inches to squeeze through. She turned sideways and eased her way through. She was cut, scratched, and gouged over the ten-meter span, but in the end, she staggered free, and she could now see the castle that the drakes were circling. Styra paused for a moment, and then, she headed for the castle.

In the solid world, seconds had passed, but here, it took hours for her to hike to the castle. She was virtually sweaty and a little tired when she got to the castle and pulled on the chain to open the portcullis.

Styra stepped into the castle and didn't flinch when the portcullis slammed down behind her. That was what it was supposed to do.

She sprinted up to the tower and climbed the endless wave of steps that were required to get her to the royal chamber. Styra looked around and blinked. There was something awry with the sleeping beauty. He was tall, he was dark purple, and he definitely wasn't provided by the scenario.

She pressed her right hand to her left wrist. "Identify situation."

The computer's voice spoke in her ear. *"Client determined that the offered female wasn't suitable. Computer replaced the projection with the client."*

Styra groaned. "Right. I will wake him up."

She walked over to him and put a hand on his shoulder. "Captain Yr-el. Please wake up."

He was cool, and as she watched, stars moved on his skin. The leather straps across his chest were definitely not the standard clothing that the computer issued. Nor was the long skirt that wrapped at his hips and went straight to his ankles. The computer had turned him into the princess.

She shook him again and then gripped her left arm. "Computer. What is stopping the client from waking?"

"Client is awaiting completion of the scenario."

"Fucking fantastic." She groaned and looked him over. He was huge. There was nowhere to kneel on the edge of the dais, and she couldn't reach his lips by leaning over, so she was going to hope that she had good reflexes when he started to wake.

8

She took a few tries but ended up plastered on top of him with her arms supporting her weight near his head. His hair was a silky black, and his brows and lashes matched.

Styra looked at the strong line of his lips and quickly pressed her lips to his with her eyes squinched shut. She lifted her head. Nothing.

She rolled to one side and activated communication. "Computer, kiss was administered, no response."

"Kiss of true love must be administered for no less than ten seconds."

"Fucking fantastic," she muttered.

She looked at him and rolled back to lying flat on him. She lowered her weight to her elbows and cursed Mr. Blue and all his scaly glory. He was so going to pay for this rescue.

She looked at the captain, and then, she pressed her lips to his, moving across his mouth to coax him into participating.

She was counting until she got to seven, where she felt his mouth move under hers. His tongue eased along her lips, and she froze until she tasted him, groaning mentally at her chance to put on the aura of a staff member.

He threaded his hand through her hair and held her as he continued the kiss. She dueled tongues with him while he stroked a hand down her back and cupped her ass. That was it. She squeaked and pushed away from him, meeting his silver and amused gaze.

"Hmm. I didn't think you were supposed to resist."

She blushed. "I am a staff member. I needed to wake you, and that meant following the scenario protocols, more or less."

He smiled. "You are real?"

She swallowed. "Yes. Well, this is a projection, just like your body is."

To her complete shock, he kissed her

again, tasting her and holding her head with both hands. His tongue twisted around hers in a fascinating way. Yes, it was a simulation, but it was a simulation of something that his mind knew very well.

Her body was humming with heat as he took his time exploring every inch of her mouth, and he seemed to be memorizing the taste of her.

She pressed her hands to his chest, and then, she thumped on him. He parted their lips in surprise.

"Sir, if you are done, we need to get you out of here. You have been in too long."

He blinked in surprise and then smiled slowly. "Fair enough, but you will have to get his agreement as well."

He nodded his head to the side, and she slowly turned to look in that direction, jolting in surprise as the head of a drake was looking at them from a few meters away. The body was clinging to the exterior of the tower, and the head had extended in via the balcony. The body was the same midnight purple as the man she was lying on, but the eyes were a bright crimson.

She gripped her arm and said, "Computer, what is the drake's part in the scenario?"

"The drake is a segment of the client. It requires a kiss to complete its scenario. A princess costume is highly effective."

"Fucking hell." She carefully got away from the client, and she focused on her appearance. She closed her eyes, and when she opened them, she was wearing a coronet and a gown that was just thick enough to make her limbs vague.

As she walked toward the drake, the gown was whipped by the wind, and the panels of fabric that were held in place by a gold chain and small pins at her shoulders went flying about, exposing a lot of skin to her original target and her new one.

She walked up to the drake, and she bowed deeply. The head extended, and the nostrils flexed and snuffled as they took in her scent. She shivered as the casual brushes of the hard beak at the tip of his head bumped and dragged across her breasts.

"So, he gets a translucent gown, and I got a bodysuit?" The captain's voice was amused.

She put her palms out and extended them toward the drake. The drake's tongue lashed out, and he then pressed against her body and whined.

She frowned. "I don't understand."

The captain's voice was amused. "He wants you on your feet with your legs apart. He's missing a scent for his collection."

She got to her feet, and the nostril

pressed against the juncture of her thighs, inhaling wildly.

Strya's cheeks were blushing, but this was all virtual and part of the job. If she had to get two parts of him out, she would.

"And now, the drake is going to kiss you."

She frowned and yelped in surprise when the drake wrapped the tip of its tongue around her ankle, widened her stance, and then ran that same tongue up her leg and inner thigh, delving into her with shocking dexterity. Her knees buckled, and a hand wrapped around her waist. "Easy, just count to ten."

She counted with every stroke, every slide, and she was nearly on the edge of orgasm when it concluded. Styra was panting, and the captain was holding her up. "Easy now, he's gotten his maiden. He's content to leave."

She nodded. "Right. Well, did you

want to leave from here? Or walk back to the entry point?"

He smiled. "I believe that we can take a short cut. Your suitor here would be happy to give you a ride."

She blushed, and the drake's eyes flashed silver before returning to crimson. It undulated up the tower and presented its neck. The captain didn't give her an option, he picked her up and took up a seat on the drake, near the base of the thick neck. Once they were in place, the drake spread its wings and simply fell across the landscape, gliding back toward the entry point. The moment that they landed, she grabbed her wrist before the captain could say anything to her. "End scenario, eject clients."

Chapter Two

Styra sat up and hit the com, "Mr. Blue, are they out?"

"They?"

"Him and his drake. Two minds, one body. You could have warned me."

"Confirmed. They have been released and are on their way to recovery." He chuckled. "Huh. I had no idea that he was an activated hybrid."

She shuddered and started to pull off her sensors and remove the filament. "He was very active."

"Well, you earned your spa day. I would take it today. You sound tense."

She groaned. "Right. Have you registered me with the spa?"

"Of course. Just walk in and do your biometrics. A day of snacks and pampering awaits."

She grinned and went to remove the sensor suit. "Thanks for holding up your end of the deal, but I am still going to penalize you for setting me up to be groped by a drake."

"What?"

"Never mind. I am going to try and enjoy the rest of my day off in peace." She sighed. "Or as much peace as I can get out here."

"Styra?"

She had her suit opened to the waist. "What?"

"Thank you."

She paused. "You are welcome. Just verify their time compression, and everything should be good."

"Already done. It is as I expected."

Styra nodded and headed off to the changing room and finished hanging up the sensor suit before she got back into her grubby exercise gear. She took her passes and left the entertainment center. Knowing Mr. Blue, she was probably on a timed pass. If she didn't check into the spa soon, she was going to lose her spot.

She turned up at the spa and smiled. "I believe Mr. Blue has called ahead."

The rest was a flurry of getting her into a comfy robe with her clothing stored; she was to have everything she wanted, and she opted to start with a full-body massage.

Thirty minutes later, she was getting a serious massage when there was a flurry of activity among the staff. Face down on the table, she muttered, "What's going on?"

Her masseur left and came back in. "A group from the imperial warship came in, and they are taking over our facility for the day. All clients are being offered

18

complete refunds and are being asked to leave the facility."

She groaned and threw a small tantrum, kicking her feet. "Of course. Well, thanks for the ten minutes. It was great."

She sat up and flexed the arm that frequently went numb from an old injury. "At least I can move it."

Fennor paused and said, "Just a minute. Don't leave."

He came back with a smug expression. "I have a compromise, but you have to share this space."

"Seriously?"

"Seriously. Come on, lie back down. We will get you moving again." Fennor oiled up his bright green hands, and when he was ready, she lay back down and kicked her sheet into position. She was moaning slightly as Fennor's fingers dug into the scar tissue on her right arm. The footsteps and soft voices were dismissed. She was in a haze of pain as her body fought the massage.

"How long has it been, Styra?"

"About three months. I have been busy." She grunted and kept herself facing downward as he straightened and flexed her arm to check the motion.

"Right. I will come back to that later. You are going to bruise."

He carefully placed her arm at her side and covered it up. Fennor continued to work on her, but he paused. "I have to get some more of the medicinal oil."

She nodded and sighed.

From the other bed in the room where another masseur was working on the other client came a familiar voice. "You have injuries."

If her arm wasn't completely numb, she would have slapped herself in the face. She lifted and turned her head. "I did. Now I have damage."

"I see. Those are blade marks." The captain was staring at her. In person, the purple of his skin was striking.

"Yeah, there is blaster scarring, too, which you might see when I roll over. So, you might want to avert your eyes at that point." She swallowed.

"I have seen damage before."

She nodded. "Right. Of course. I am sorry to have intruded on your stress relief."

"I believe I should be apologizing. It seems that your need was far greater than ours."

She blushed. "It isn't a problem. I will be out of here as soon as Fennor has me mobile again."

He leaned up on his elbows. "You had a day planned here?"

"Yes."

"Then, enjoy it. We can stay out of your way."

She looked at Gemb, who was working on the captain. He gave her a smile and a nod.

"Um, sure. If you don't mind. That would be helpful."

Fennor came back with the deep-heating rub, and he got back to work.

She placed her face through the cutout in the bed, and she grunted, moaned, and groaned with every bit of therapeutic handling.

"Okay, Styra, roll over." Fennor moved between her and the captain and held up the sheet so she could roll away from the intense silver gaze.

She flopped into position, and he tucked the sheet over her, and he started working on her arm.

The captain's side of the room was silent. It was as if Gemb wasn't able to work any of the tissue under the skin.

"So, are you and your ship staying long?" She glanced at him.

"A few more days. We are awaiting a personnel transfer."

That made sense. It was common

enough on Blue Station. They were in a great position for folk to come together from around the nearest six star systems.

Fennor tugged her sheet down and draped a shorter sheet across her breasts while he worked on the mess that had been made of her abdomen.

He was leaning up to look. "You took a point-blank blast to the torso."

She nodded. "I am aware of it."

"The scars are pale. How old were you?"

She grimaced. "Six. Raider attack. Out of a ship with two hundred people, I was one of nine survivors." She anticipated his questions. "We floated into a shipping lane, and from there, I was brought to the med center here. I grew up on this station."

He was shocked. "The station master raised you?"

"More or less. He hired a nanny for me and told me he would take it out of my

23

future earnings." She smiled. "I have a very thorough and strange education."

"I see. I did not realize that Mr. Blue was so generous as to take in humans."

She grunted as Fennor hit the knot that kept her from standing straight most days. Sweat appeared on her forehead, and she shook as she fought the urge to punch her therapist and run for it.

"You are in pain." The captain's voice was tense.

She gritted her teeth and nodded. "Yeah, there are issues with muscle attachments in the wrong place. They tighten up over time, and since I have been busy with work, I have left it too long. The price I pay for easy motion."

Fennor muttered, "Almost done."

The twang of the freed tendon was a bolt of pain that she wasn't expecting. She shrieked, and tears ran from her eyes.

She sobbed for a minute, and Fennor

24

went on to her legs, and then, he covered her up, patted her shoulder, and said, "Take the time you need."

She nodded and slowly let the aches and pains become her body again. She swallowed and glanced at the captain, he was on his back now, and his expression was completely appalled.

She wrapped the sheet around her and waddled over to where she had her robe. She slid her arms into it and let the sheet drop. She returned the sheet to the bed and bowed toward the captain. "I am sorry for disturbing your time. Thank you for your patience."

She left via the back door and headed for the sauna. She changed her robe for a wrap as she heard masculine voices coming from the sauna.

When she opened the door, the six men went silent, so she chuckled. "Apologies. As you were."

She found a corner and sat as

comfortably as she was able, slumping down onto the seat with her hands loose in her lap. She kept her eyes closed, and gradually the voices resumed their discussion of the trip to the entertainment center. Apparently, they had all had a very good time. They didn't remember much except thrills, danger, and then satisfaction, but that was the effect of the center. No one remembered how the adventures turned out, except for folks like herself who had to remain cognizant of everything before and after. There were only a handful of women on the station who had that training, but she was one of them.

When they started speculating on the adventure that the captain had had, she kept herself as still as possible. Apparently, he had come out of it energized with a smile on his face that both intrigued and chilled them. He tended to wear that expression when he was trying to out-think an opponent.

She suddenly wasn't getting the benefit from the sauna that she thought she would get. The hot tub held far more appeal.

She quietly got up and slipped out of the sauna, turned toward the hot tub, and froze. There was a wall in the way, and it was breathing.

She looked up and met his curious expression. "Excuse me, please."

"Where are you going?"

She smiled. "Just a hot soak. The jets might be kinder to me than passive heat."

He paused and nodded. "I will accompany you."

Styra's eyes went wide. "It is not necessary. You . . . your men . . . um . . . I have nothing."

He smiled, and a low chuckle emerged. "Good. It is settled. Which way do we go?"

She nodded toward the hall behind

him, and he turned sideways so she could lead the way.

She could feel the wall of heat that he radiated at her back and part of her relaxed. He had already seen the damage, and she hadn't yet run into the man who would take on the twisted-up mess than she lived in. She was a curiosity, which wasn't flattering, but it made for a solid base when dealing with folks naked.

She made it to the hot tub area, walked to a chair, and slipped off her robe, walking to the tub and slowly climbing down the steps before looking at the captain. He shed his own robe and stepped into the tub, settling down next to her before smiling and leaning back.

"So, why don't you put your scars on your virtual presence?"

She had been relaxing in the warm water, and she froze, turning to meet his bright and amused gaze. She swallowed and thought about answering him when

his eyes flared red.
   Oh, shit.

Chapter Three

"What do you mean?" Ignorance seemed the best way to go.

He explained. "When you were wearing the gown, there was no trace of scarring, and you moved easily. Why don't you wear yourself in the scenarios?"

She trembled and tried to keep calm. "I take the form of my best day. I don't wear the scars because I have a whole limb to compare. I move easily because three days from now, when the bruising subsides, I will have a few days without pain, and I remember how that feels because it feels good. That is who I want to be in the scenarios, so that is who I am."

He moved closer to her. "Why did you

wear the dress for him?"

Styra watched his eyes flicker in colour. "Um, in the scenarios, drakes have to be confronted by maidens or princesses. The computer has clothing on file for me for each scenario."

"And for my portion of the scenario? No additional clothing was required?"

She smiled. "The bodysuit was close enough to armor for the computer. For you, the kiss was the most important part."

He had moved so close that if she shifted her arm, he would be touching her. She slumped down in the water so that the churning of the surface hid her.

"Was it?"

He leaned down to kiss her, and his lips were millimeters away when he raised his head, and a frightening expression came over his features, his eyes crimson.

She sat up and looked in the direction

he was focused on. Oh, it was his men.

She elbowed him under the water. He blinked and straightened. "What was that for?"

"You looked like you were going to start breathing fire."

They finished talking, and his men joined them. Well, they almost joined them. The captain glared at them and jerked his head, so his men chose a separate hot tub, far down the chamber.

Styra frowned at him. "You didn't have to do that. I can leave."

"The heat is an important part of your therapy, yes?"

She drew the answer out. "Yeesssss?"

"Then, you shall remain here until you have what you need, and I will keep you company."

Her laugh rang out. "You don't exactly inspire relaxation."

His expression was hurt. "Why not?"

"You are just . . ." She waved a wet

hand at him. "You. Intimidating as hell."

"It is useful in most situations." He frowned.

"I am sure. It is just not very relaxing."

He scowled at her and then seemed to come to a decision. He picked her up and seated her across his lap before kissing her.

What the fuck?

She held her breath as his tongue teased at hers, and when she opened her lips slightly, he slid in. He tasted just like he did in the scenario. She shivered, and he wrapped an arm around her waist, and the other cupped her jaw. His grip was delicate, but she knew that if she tried to get away, she would be in for a bit of an issue.

The conversation from the other tub had ceased, but she focused on the taste of the captain in real life and the feel of the heat from his skin to hers.

She pressed her hand to his chest and

felt the very slow and heavy thud of his heart.

He continued the slow kiss for what could have been minutes or could have been hours, all she knew was that her lips were humming and tingling when he raised his head. He smiled slowly. "Still intimidated?"

"Um . . . that isn't the word for it."

He turned her so that her back was pressed against his chest, and he wrapped his arms around her under the water.

"What do you normally do around the station?" He whispered it in her ear.

She swallowed. Normally, she would spend the day after a massage in bed, but she wasn't going to say that. "I go and watch a vid, go to the gym—but I did that this morning—or go to dinner."

"Hmm. Will you go to dinner with me?"

He waited.

"Uh, yes?"

He chuckled. "You don't sound confident."

"I am not. Unless I am in the scenarios, confidence is not my strong suit."

She looked in the water at the contrast between his dark purple skin and her pearl white. Mr. Blue had told her that she was human but damaged. She didn't quite believe him because all of the humans that she knew didn't glow softly in the dark. Mr. Blue had also told her that she wasn't compatible with any of the races that visited the station, including humans. It was a bit of a contradiction that didn't really matter. Her body was too jacked-up for more than a quick glance anyway. *Wait, so why is he . . .*

She shifted slightly, and his erection was definitely against her back. From his vantage point, he could see the worst of the damage. Apparently, for him, it was not a turn-off.

Her body was in shock at the possibility that his attraction presented. Her body was going to ache like hell tomorrow, so she had one day to do something. Maybe.

"How long is your ship going to be here?"

"Three or four days. Why?" His whisper was hot in her ear.

She couldn't say it. "It doesn't matter."

"I think it does, but I will not press you."

She held up her hands. "I had better get out. I am getting all pruney."

His arms didn't release her. "I don't want you to go."

She chuckled. "I am just going back to the sauna now that it is quiet."

He touched her chin with a wet hand and turned her head toward him. "One more kiss."

He leaned over her, and his lips met hers in a kiss that sent waves of heat tearing through her. She clutched the hand cupping her jaw and met his tongue with her own but with less twisting dexterity. She was gasping and moaning, her body was throbbing, and he had only had contact with her mouth. When he raised his head, his eyes were red, and his smile was smug.

"Now, you can go."

She didn't want to say that she wasn't sure her legs would carry her, but she turned her head away from him and made her way to the steps by a force of will. She got out of the water, toweled off as if she didn't have an audience, and then, she slipped on her robe again and walked down the hall to the sauna room.

She stopped at the water dispenser and drank a few cups before heading into the sauna.

Once she was alone inside, she took off her robe and sat on it, shivering as her body slowly came down from its sensitization. She stretched her body out on the bench and groaned. Styra wanted to punch something.

She had waited years for someone compatible to come along, and now, if she took advantage, she would only have him for a few days! So, was she better off with ignoring the attraction that seemed to be reciprocal, or should she just wrap herself around him and go for it?

She growled and kicked her feet flat against the bench. Yes, it was a tantrum, but she definitely deserved the opportunity to pitch a fit.

She panted and sat back up, draping the robe over her shoulders. She leaned back and let the heat do its job for twenty minutes before she put her arms through the sleeves and headed to the tepid shower.

She scrubbed, exfoliated, and stood under the spray with her hands braced against the wall.

Styra turned to see the captain watching her. The red of his gaze gave her a general idea of where his thoughts had been roaming. She sighed. "That is very creepy."

He shrugged. "I just left the hot tub and was headed for a shower myself. Are all the facilities here, unisex?"

She nodded. "Yes. They just have a stringent *no sex in public* policy. They enforce it."

"So, that is why you are just standing there?" He cocked his head.

Fuck! She headed for the towel rack and wrapped one of the sheets around her. "To be honest, it really hasn't been an issue before."

He grinned. "Local men must be idiots."

"No. They are not compatible." She clapped her hand over her mouth, turned, and headed for a fresh robe.

She put on the robe and tied the sash a

moment before she was certain he was right behind her.

"Compatible?"

"Just something Mr. Blue used to tell me." She swallowed. "Please, excuse me." She ducked away from him and headed for the snack area. All of these extra calories burned were making her hungry.

She was the only person in the snack area. She ordered her meal, a few beverages, and then she went to have a seat with the star scape spinning above her. One of the staff members came up to her with the drink order and assured her that her meal would be out in a few minutes.

She sipped at her tea and then surrendered to what her body was demanding. She curled her right arm up against her body and draped it across her breasts, hanging onto her left side while she sipped her tea. It looked odd, but it was comfortable and kept her muscles from tightening up again.

She looked up at the stars and smiled. All her life in space and she had never travelled beyond the confines of the station.

She heard the men laughing and chatting with each other as they paused and placed their meal orders. She glanced over at them, and the captain wasn't with them.

The crew came over to the table next to hers, and as they pulled out their chairs, they bowed and said, "Ma'am."

She chuckled. She was younger than all of them, but she felt immeasurably older. "Where did *he* go?"

The men looked at each other, and one said, "He had to take a meeting."

She smiled, and one of the men asked, "Ma'am, do you work at the entertainment center?"

She chuckled. "Only when things go wrong."

They looked at each other, and one of

them said, "Then, where did you meet Captain Yr-el?"

Styra shrugged, and she was frank. "I met him in his scenario. Things went wrong."

Chapter Four

Yr-el glared at the other drake. "Mbrak, what the hell did you do?"

Mbrak smiled slightly. "What do you mean?"

He walked toward the full drake with menace. "You could have healed the damage to Styra easily."

"No, only if I took her as mate. She and I are not compatible, so I simply made sure she had the maximum amount of medical care at our disposal."

Yr-el growled. "What do you mean, *not compatible*?"

Mbrak sighed. "I mean that five generations ago, I fathered a child with a human, and it became her ancestor. It was when I was young and stupid, but she is my offspring, a few generations removed."

"Why didn't you get her a mate who could help her before this?" Yr-el was slightly less enraged at the obvious years of pain that his female had been through.

Mbrak snorted. "I have been trying. Do you know how hard it is to find a drake descendant with enough energy to heal someone with as much damage as she has? Half her organs are missing for the love of the first egg!"

"So, you lured me here?"

Mbrak grinned with bared teeth. "I did. Oh, there is still a personnel exchange for your empire, I just made sure that they were a little late and you were already here."

"What if I had a mate already?"

Mbrak snorted. "I did my homework. Don't be so outraged. I did what was necessary for my blood kin. Some of the others here are in the same situation, but they are in good health."

Yr-el paused. "You have other descendants here?"

"Certainly. Five of them. They run the entertainment center for me, and they all start on companion missions, so sex isn't a mystery to them." Mbrak shrugged. "I have mates on the way for two of them."

"You are using your station to matchmake for your descendants?" Yr-el was stunned.

"Of course. What else would I use it for?" Mbrak chuckled. "Your father would be amused. His mate was floating alone in a stasis pod in the middle of his sector. He literally snagged her out of space and took her home with him. He had no idea that she was compatible until they were together for the first time. His dragon knew, but Harmoth had no idea."

Yr-el snorted. "Yes, I know."

"Well, what did your dragon say about

45

Styra?"

Yr-el shuddered. "He is in favour of her."

Mbrak was smug. "So, you return to the depths of the spa, and I will return to my command center. If she will accept you, take her. If she lets you heal her, I wish you nothing but centuries of enjoyment."

"You think she will not?"

"I think that she has lived a long time in pain. Sometimes the thought of freedom is more frightening than a life in agony."

Yr-el nodded and turned before he turned back. "What happened to the raiders?"

"Ah, they were hard to digest, but their ship made lovely sparkles as I fired it into a sun."

Yr-el nodded. "Good. One less task."

Mbrak nodded, and they parted ways.

Yr-el returned to the spa, and he used

his senses to track Styra through the building. He found her easily, having a meal and chatting easily with the crew of the long-distance shuttle that he had flown to the station.

His lieutenant jumped to his feet. "Captain, may I get you something?"

He nodded. "Thank you. Anything is suitable."

He headed over to the counter, and the staff member nodded.

Yr-el pulled a chair out next to Styra, and he smiled. "So, how long have you worked with Mbrak?"

She sighed. "You were talking to him."

"I was."

"I have worked for him since I became an adult, well, in the entertainment center. I have been working on designing scenarios since I was twelve."

One of the men choked. "Twelve?"

She grinned. "Not all of the scenarios involve sex. Some are simply action-

47

adventure or solitary days watching the sunrise or sunset."

His men looked exponentially relieved.

She chuckled at their expressions. "Mr. Blue doesn't allow inappropriate behaviour around the scenarios. Everything has to be done with the consent of both parties or with a computer simulation."

The captain chuckled. "I believe some of the men just had mild coronaries."

Styra smiled. "I noticed. When I was younger, I specialized in landscapes. One of the other ladies worked on designing alternate characters for clients to interact with. There are a bunch of us behind the scenes that no one thinks are there. We pop into scenarios, check on how things are progressing, and verify that the client is maintaining the guidelines."

One of the men asked, "So, what happened with Captain Yr-el?"

Styra looked at him, and he shrugged

his compliance. "Um, he found the female in the simulation unsuitable, so the computer improvised and switched things around. Mr. Blue called me in on my day off, and I had to go in and get him loose from the scenario."

The men were disappointed.

The captain provided more detail. "I was on a quest to find a damsel who was waiting for a kiss. I wasn't impressed with the simulation and didn't follow the projected actions, so the computer switched me for the princess. I was out for about ten minutes in live time, six hours in the simulation."

The guys looked at each other, and the lieutenant asked, "How do you remember the details?"

The captain gave them a bland look. "I have a different relationship with time."

One of the others asked, "How did you get out of it?"

The captain started to eat the food that

had just arrived. "That was simple, she kissed me."

Styra felt it necessary to explain. "The computer has protocols that have to be met in order to release a client."

The captain paused, "And then she had to kiss the dragon."

She covered her eyes at the shocked expressions of his men. The lieutenant let out a strangled, "She had to kiss it?"

"Well, *he* kissed *her*. Even for a simulation, he was very impressed with her."

She fought the shudder that wanted to run through her. The memory of the tongue was just a memory, but it was vivid. Her face felt like it was on fire, but the thick skin of her face didn't really discolour unless bruised.

She reached for the teacup, and she rattled it before she was able to pick it up.

The youngest of the crewmen frowned. "Was it upsetting?"

She sipped, swallowed, and set her cup

down. "It was . . . unexpected."

The captain chuckled, and he continued to eat his meal.

The staff cleared the dishes as the group finished, and Styra nodded for them to take the remainder of her plate.

The captain frowned. "Why didn't you finish it?"

She chuckled. "I can't. Eating is kind of a form of entertainment for me, but I can't digest any of the nutrients."

He stared at her in shock. "How do you live like that?"

Styra smiled. "I am not fond of the alternative. Mr. Blue gets me the supplements that I need, and he gets paid in labour. It's how we do things around here."

She slowly lowered her right arm and forced herself not to wince. "Well, this has been an interesting afternoon, gentlemen. I hope that you enjoy your time on the station."

The captain grabbed her arm as she

passed. "We will still be having dinner."

She didn't say what she was thinking; instead, she smiled. "Of course."

"I will contact you via Mbrak."

She nodded. "Fine. Okay."

His thumb rubbed along her arm, and he smiled. "Have a good day."

She nodded, and she walked away when he finally let her go. She didn't look back but headed for the change room. She awkwardly pulled her exercise clothing on and grabbed her passes, and headed for her quarters. She needed her muscle relaxants and her supplements. If she wasn't mistaken, she had a date.

Mr. Blue called her at six. "Styra, he is waiting for you at the Artuth."

"Um. Okay."

The screen went from audio to video. He looked at her with concern. "Are you all right?"

"A little off balance. This hasn't

happened before."

He cocked his head. "Would it be acceptable to consider it a scenario?"

She smiled and shook her head. "That wouldn't be fair to either of us. No, I am going to see him, and we will see where things go."

Mr. Blue smiled. "Good attitude. You look lovely, by the way."

She nodded. "Thank you. Getting my hair up was a nightmare."

He frowned. "Is your arm bothering you?"

"Fennor worked me over today. He does good work, but he doesn't spare the tissue."

"Ah. Well, have a nice evening, and if you feel you can trust Yr-el, do it."

She smiled. "I guess that is what it comes down to. Right. I had better go. Thanks, Mr. Blue."

He sighed. "You can address me properly."

She winked. "I am not calling you Grandpa. It feels weird."

He laughed, and they disconnected the link.

She looked herself over in the mirror. The dress was similar to the one she wore in the scenario. Her bodice was a crisscrossing of lacing, the dress was three layers of filmy material that just managed to hide the colour of her nipples, and the sandals were practical. Her sleeves covered most of her scars and were open from the elbow down.

She had fought her hair into a coronet, and she felt reasonably attractive. With a deep breath, she headed out of her quarters and took a few of the gliding sidewalks to the Artuth. It was a lovely restaurant, and she wished that she could do the meals justice. Ah well, she could taste them.

Styra walked into the restaurant, and she didn't even have a chance to explain who she was meeting when she was guided through the tables to a private room through an elaborate archway.

The door was opened for her, and the captain was there, dressed in a manner very similar to what he had been wearing in the scenario. *Oh, fuck.*

He smiled slowly and walked over to her. "Styra, you look . . . amazing."

She nodded. "You look terrifyingly attractive yourself."

He took her hands in his and pressed a soft kiss to her lips. When he raised his head, he smiled. "It seemed appropriate."

She looked down at her own dress and up again. "Same here."

He squeezed her hands. "Come and have a seat. I have arranged a meal to be consumed over the next three hours."

She stared at him. "Three hours?"

"I got details about your condition from Mbrak, so I spoke to the chef, and we worked out a plan so that you can enjoy your evening."

Styra needed to get to work early in the morning, but if she was careful, she might be able to get enough sleep before tomorrow morning and her routine of injections and painkillers.

He walked to a sliding wall and escorted her to a second chamber with a low table and cushions on the floor. She knelt on one of the cushions, and he didn't sit across from her but sat next to her. The server came in through a panel that was barely visible and set a tea set out as well as a small carafe of wine with a large glass and a small glass.

She looked at it and grinned. "This looks like it is going to be fun."

He smiled. "I certainly hope you enjoy it."

The first course emerged, and it was one small item on a very small plate for her, and a larger version of the same for him. Styra chuckled and dove in. It was a once-in-a-lifetime meal and her first proper date. She wasn't going to let the opportunity to enjoy herself pass her by.

Chapter Five

After the second hour, Styra was giggling with every question. She really shouldn't have had the third thimble of wine.

"I see that I forgot to ask Mbrak about your alcohol tolerance." Yr-el shook his head.

She blinked. "Oh. I have an excellent tolerance, just not when I have had to use injectors just so I can move." She wrinkled her nose. "Huh. I wasn't going to tell you about that."

He snorted. "Well, if that is all it is, I can fix that, but it might hurt."

She stared at him, not sure if she had heard him correctly. "You can fix what?"

"Your injuries. The pain. My particular bloodline has a regenerative skill. I believe that is why Mbrak lured me here."

His eyes were silver and serious, the light moved under his skin, and she watched stars move and collide. She really wanted to follow some of the light with her fingertips, but she curled her hands into her lap instead.

She swallowed. "I wouldn't want to inconvenience you. It seems that Mr. Blue has already done enough."

He cocked his head. "You will not ask me for assistance?"

She shrugged. "I am used to it. It is fine. It is how I schedule my time."

He blinked. "You don't want a life pain-free?"

She chuckled. "I don't know what I would do with it."

"Perhaps, think of something else to do with your time spent managing pain?"

"Like what?"

He smiled, and his elegant features were charming. "Like me."

Her face and specific parts of her body went hot. "Oh."

She met his gaze. "I wouldn't consider that a full-time occupation."

He snorted in surprise. "I don't know whether to be amused or insulted."

When he moved, she could see the muscles of his abdomen bunch and relax. She slowly looked up, and he was watching her stare at him. He reached over and pulled her into his lap. "I believe I will opt for amused."

He tugged at her neckline and eased her dress off her shoulder. "If you are numbed to pain, this might not be as difficult as it would otherwise be, but it isn't going to be pleasant."

"Here?"

"You wish to wait? I thought proof of concept would help you along." He flexed his fingers, and the tabs that connected

60

her sleeve came away, one by one.

"What if someone comes?" she slapped her left hand to her chest to keep the dress from exposing her breast.

"There is not a course scheduled for another thirty minutes." He pressed a kiss to her shoulder. "We have privacy."

She looked at his dark head, and she swallowed. "What does this entail?"

He left a trail of kisses down her arm, the exposed and twisted skin. "A little blood calling to blood."

She blinked at the feel of his lips against the basically numbed skin. She watched, and he slowly traced his tongue along the lines of the scars. When he had traced all the ones in that bundle, he lifted his hand and drew his thumb across his palm. Blood ran down onto her arm, and it faithfully followed the wet trace left by his tongue.

She watched the blood run along her skin until it covered everywhere that he

61

had licked. He lifted his hand to his mouth and licked the wound. While she watched, the slice closed.

When he kissed her, she widened her eyes because she could taste far more than copper along his tongue. She wanted to ask him what was going on, but he threaded a hand through her hair, and he held her to the kiss while the taste slowly dissipated. His tongue moved along hers, swirled, and plunged, and she shifted her thighs together as there was a reaction.

He lifted his head and closed his eyes. "Take a deep breath."

She didn't know what was going on, but there was a wrenching pain in her arm while he held her tight. She looked down, and there was light coming from the scar tissue. Her arm throbbed, and the muscles twisted as alignments were shaped and formed once again.

She was covered in sweat, panting,

and ten minutes had passed before the pain subsided. She was gasping for air, and she didn't want to look at her arm.

He pressed a kiss to her temple and licked the sweat. "You can look at it. Your arm is still there."

She looked over, and her arm was, indeed, still there. Her sleeve was down, the metallic white of her skin was glowing, and there were only slight marks left from the original scars. The muscle looked the same as her other side. "How did you do that?"

"My father's skill. Blood healing. The blast damage will have to be addressed over a few days. Doing it in one would be dangerous for you."

She blinked. "You will only be here a few more days."

He smiled. "Then, I suppose we will have to make alternative arrangements."

She flexed her hand and raised her arm. "It feels like it does in the scenarios.

63

Thank you." She looked at him and beamed.

He cuddled her and smiled. "I have never found this technique to be particularly useful before now. It is too slow for use in battle."

She flexed her hand again. "I am sorry it isn't more useful, but I can only say that I am grateful for it."

He stroked her jaw and tilted her head toward him. "I believe I have discovered its true purpose."

Styra didn't ask what he was talking about, she was too busy closing her eyes as he kissed her slowly, lifting her up to face him. She draped her arms around his neck before she paused and reached down to yank on the front panels of her skirt. When her legs were free of the fabric, she moved toward him, leaning against his chest and relaxing slightly.

She heard the door open and continued kissing the captain until the server left. She leaned back, and she looked away in embarrassment. He tilted her back, and his lips moved across the exposed breast that she had forgotten about.

The freedom to cover her face with both hands was definitely new. His chuckle was felt as well as heard while he licked and sucked at her nipple. He slid his hand into the parting of her skirt, and he paused, pressing his forehead against her collarbone. "You aren't wearing anything else."

She swallowed. "The skirt catches if I wear anything under it."

His fingers were pressed against her, and she was slick. She could feel it. He slipped a finger into her, and she froze at the unfamiliar feeling. Sure, she had toys but nothing that moved along the front wall and searched out that particular spot. Her breath caught in her lungs as he ran the pad of his finger over that inner spot, and she twisted against his hand, pushing at his shoulders. She opened her eyes a tiny bit, and his eyes were crimson as he watched her ride his hand.

She held onto him when she bucked, and the nearly painful tension expanded and encompassed her body.

It took four slow seconds before she relaxed against him, and he curled her up against him. He kissed her and smiled, withdrawing his finger from her and sliding it into his mouth before his eyes flickered back to silver.

It took a few tries before she could speak, and she whispered, "Why do your eyes change?"

He shrugged. "He wants a better view."

She remembered the hot look in the scaled features, and she swallowed. "Oh."

He stroked a hand down her back.

Styra swallowed and glanced toward the table. A slightly melted fruit dessert was waiting for them on the table. She chuckled. "Will you let me reach the sweets?"

He leaned forward, still holding her, and gathered her cup and the tiny spoon. It was gone in seconds, and she sighed sadly as she looked at his normal-sized dessert. The fruit mousse had been very good.

He touched her chin and tried to lift it for a kiss, but her gaze was fixed on the mousse.

He chuckled. "Do you really want it that bad?"

She focused on him. "Yes. Yes, I do."

He reached for it and took the cup and spoon, handing it over to her. She wiggled happily and ate two bites, sighing in enjoyment. "Thank you."

Yr-el blinked. "That is it?"

"Yes. I know when things are enough. I also know when they are not enough."

He smiled. "What about me?"

She looked away in embarrassment. "More than enough."

He chuckled and took the dessert from her, eating it with raised brows. "It is good, but you are sweeter."

She blinked.

"And creamier."

Her hands slammed over her face again. That was not an analysis that she had ever faced.

He leaned over and set the glass back on the table, running his hands over her back until she peeped out from between her fingers.

"One more course, and then, I would like you to come to my rooms so I can personally examine your injury. I haven't had a chance to properly check the levels of damage."

She was taken aback at the sudden change from seduction to analysis. "Oh. Um, okay. I can bring up the med scans."

He smiled. "That will be helpful."

She pulled her dropped dress up and held it up to cover her. Thankfully the other side of her dress was still in place, so with a little bit of tugging, she was able to arrange it into a cover that didn't need to be monitored while she was sitting still.

She tried to lean toward her seat, but he casually settled her with him sitting cross-legged and her nestled between his thighs. She was facing the table, and he had his arms wrapped around her. She wasn't in danger of getting away.

She settled against him and relaxed. It was quite a trick considering the erection she could feel under the layers of fabric between them. They sat in silence until the staff member came in to remove their dessert cups and leave a tea set behind.

She closed her eyes at the scent and smiled, leaning for it and then being brought up short by his arms. She huffed. "Can you just let me pour?"

He reached out and pulled the table to them. "I like you where you are."

Styra snorted as she reached out to pour the two cups of minty brew. She handed one to him and then took the other for herself. She leaned back against him and sipped at the tiny cup. "Thank you for this evening. It was . . . nice."

He chuckled. "I am glad."

She sipped at her tea, and he sipped at his.

"So, back to your accommodations after this?"

He squeezed her gently. "Yes."

She nodded. "Okay."

Sitting surrounded by him was incredibly soothing. She held her tea carefully and looked at the smoothed skin of her arm. All these years and all she needed a stunning drake and a few minutes of agony to fix it. It made her a little nervous for what was going to happen when he worked on her blast scar, but if she could actually eat a meal, run, or even exercise and breathe at the same time, she would just grit her teeth and wait for the lack of issue on the other side.

She could deal with a little—or a lot—of pain if it meant she would be able to move and behave like the rest of the crew at the entertainment center. Mr. Blue had hired them all as children and raised them together. Her injuries had stopped her from joining in the more boisterous training, so Mr. Blue had helped her compensate by aiding her in writing scenarios where she was the drake or she was running or she was flying under her own power. She could be anything, and she could do anything, as long as it was inside a scenario.

She touched the heavily embroidered fabric of the wrap skirt that Yr-el was wearing. It radiated the heat from the body underneath it.

She set her teacup down after she

finished it, and he put his next to hers. "Shall we go?"

Styra nodded, and he helped her to her feet. As he rose to his feet, she split the sleeve that was dangling uselessly, tied it in a knot, and managed to reclaim her dignity.

He nodded at her solution with a smile and took her hand in his. He walked out of the restaurant with her, and the staff bowed as they passed. That was different, but as she knew most of the staff from their time in the entertainment centers, she didn't make eye contact. Knowing their personal kinks was a burden that those who worked at the entertainment center had to bear.

As they walked through the station, Yr-el pulled her close to him. The hotel was near the entertainment center, which was great for going to work the following day if she didn't need to go back to her quarters and get her passes.

The hotel staff bowed and didn't crack a smile at her as she passed. That was different. Normally, they were up for a grin and a wave.

Styra looked up at Yr-el, and she wondered why everyone was so petrified of him. He was a lovely person who was kind and considerate.

They stepped into the lift, his hand tightened on her waist, and his eyes flashed red. *Oh. Right. The drake.*

Chapter Six

Styra looked around the luxury suite and studiously ignored the bed that had been neatly turned down.

Yr-el unbuckled the straps on his chest, and she didn't ask why he wore them to begin with. He looked and her and smiled. "You can come in. I won't bite. Not yet."

She pressed a hand to her cheek, and she tried to throttle the heat that his words sent rushing through her.

He smiled and had removed the heavy belt and the wrist cuff that he wore. "Now, I would recommend that you disrobe and get on the bed. This might make a bit of a mess."

She clutched at the silky fabric but removed it carefully and set it aside. The twist and pucker of her scar was right beneath her breasts and off to one side.

She asked, "How does one discover that one has a talent for this kind of healing?"

He smiled and walked over to her. "My father learned of it when he healed my mother. He had no idea that he could do it until he needed to, so it was a safe guess that my situation would be the same."

"Well, if this works, I will definitely be a fan for life."

He grinned and then calmed. "It will work, but it will be painful. Are you prepared?"

"Um, do you need to see my medical records?"

He shook his head. "I can read you without the scans. I can see the injury. Will you accept a little light healing?"

She nodded. "I will deal with as much

75

as you can manage. It will be better than teasing me with it in increments."

He raised his brows. "I can do that if you are sure, but you will have to take the blood in as it is more than can be contained in a kiss."

She swallowed and nodded, then paused. "I will. Wait, how will I take it in?"

He slid his hand between her thighs. "Other means."

Styra wasn't particularly startled, but she was slightly embarrassed. He was looking her over intently, and his gaze wasn't fixed on her scar.

Yr-el eased her into the center of the bed, and he then moved his head over the drawn and pulled silver skin in the center of her torso.

"This must have hurt."

She swallowed as he traced the marks with his fingertips. "Mr. Blue said that I was unconscious for weeks after they

76

found me, and the doctors had done what they could."

"This isn't the work of physicians." He looked at her with silver eyes.

Styra chuckled. "I know. Mr. Blue healed me using our grandparent-child bond, though it was weak by that point."

"So, you always knew he was a drake?"

"I can barely remember my parents, but they told me stories about the drakes and the few who had mixed with humans and the result."

"Who is your other contributor?"

She watched his finger slowly trace the shiny skin. She could feel pressure but nothing else. "Um, Akinoth."

"Ah, I have heard of him. He specializes in helping humans colonize ice worlds for research and minerals."

She nodded and watched as he began to lick and trace his tongue along the edge of her damaged skin. "I have never met him."

"Well, this healing pattern is one of his, so he has met you."

She sat up on her elbows. "What?"

"This silver snowflake pattern. This is his insignia, for lack of a better term."

"What is it for?"

"My best guess is to keep you alive."

"How would that work?"

"It formed a direct link between you and him. Interesting." He smiled. "Well, we are going to close that link tonight."

She swallowed as he traced inward in a spiral with his tongue.

When her skin was gleaming with the trail of his saliva, he looked at her and asked, "Ready?"

She nodded, and he moved away from the bed to prep a few syringes. "This will get the bulk that you need inside you."

She blinked. "I thought you were going to . . ."

"I considered it, but this will be more effective. You are missing more tissue

78

than I thought."

Styra blinked as he casually filled the syringes with his blood. "Why do you have so many syringes in your hotel room?"

He grinned. "For boring weekends."

She sensed she wasn't going to get an answer when he set the syringes neatly on a tray, and then, he scooped her up and draped her over him, with his head propped against the headboard and her body comfortably situated on top of him. Well, relatively comfortable. She was still naked, and he was half-dressed. She didn't know which combination of clothing and lack thereof she was hoping for, but lying on him like an offering wasn't ideal.

"Do you remember how the last one went?"

She nodded. "Yeah."

"This is going to be exponentially worse."

He ran his thumb along his palm again, and the drops of blood found the saliva and followed the path until an undulating puddle was sitting on top of the damage. He picked up the first of the syringes, and there was a hiss as it disgorged its contents through the edge of the scar and into the area of damage.

The other injections went just as quick. He licked his bloodied hand and kissed her again, holding her other hand. "Here we go."

She tasted blood, and something moved inside her abdomen. At first, things got hot, then there was a pulse, and then pain came in, screaming along her nerves.

White-hot pain racked her, and Yr-el took her screams until the pain faded and the popping and shifting sensation had eased. It seemed like a good time to rest.

She woke up with Yr-el washing her

hair. They were in the huge bathroom, and she was seated on a stool while his fingers massaged her scalp.

She couldn't look down with his hands controlling her head, so she slid a hand up her ribs, waiting for the hard and almost metallic feel. Normal skin was in its place. She felt the hot tears trickle down her cheeks as she inhaled deeply and exhaled, using more than just the one and a quarter lung that had previously been at her disposal.

Yr-el said, "Lean your head back."

He took a spray nozzle and carefully rinsed her hair. "You were only out for thirty minutes. Impressive."

She chuckled. "I always did bounce back quickly."

He gently moved through her hair with the jets of water. "You have a very strong constitution."

"So I have been told." She inhaled and exhaled again. "That feels so weird."

"What does?"

"Breathing."

He turned the water off and worked to wring out her hair before wrapping it in a towel. "Breathing?"

"Yeah. I don't remember the feeling of actually feeling energized while inhaling and exhaling. It has always been a bit of a fight."

He wrapped his arms around her and picked her up. The bed had been changed since she had laid down with him. She suspected that she knew the issue.

"Things got gross, huh?"

He shrugged. "It was a side effect of the pain. Nothing that couldn't be tidied up while I bathed you."

She sighed. "Sorry."

He settled her on the bed and that is when she became aware of his own lack of clothing. He curled up next to her and held her against him. "Just get some rest, Styra."

"You are not the boss of me." She mumbled it against his chest.

"Yes, I am. Today, I am definitely the boss of you." He chuckled and rubbed her back.

She wanted to pick some kind of fight, but she was exhausted.

His chest was warm, his hands were warm, she felt like she had just climbed the interior of the station, so it was time for a rest.

She woke up at her normal five in the morning. Yr-el had rolled to one side, so she slipped to the dispenser in the bathing room and ordered a bodysuit. She slipped into it in the dark, and when she crept toward the door, she heard, "Where are you off to?"

She turned, and red eyes were glowing in her direction. "I have to go to work today."

"Come here."

She walked toward him cautiously. He held out his hand and pulled her down to him. He threaded a hand into her hair and pulled her to him for a kiss.

His tongue slid along hers, and he wrapped his hand around her back and flattened her against him. She moaned and ran her hands down his chest before she realized that she had to be at work in half an hour. She pressed against his chest and broke the kiss. She gasped, "I have to get to work."

His red eyes narrowed. "I want you to stay."

"I want to stay, too, but I have to get to work. I will be free in nine hours."

He sighed. "Fine. Your passes are in the drawer next to the vid."

She blinked and stared at him. "When?"

"They were delivered here while we were at dinner. Mbrak ordered someone to bring them."

"So, he knows I was here?"

He gave her a droll look. "Of course, he did."

"Great. That won't make work awkward." She tried to pry herself free. "If I can get to work. I appear to be stuck on something."

He smiled. "One more kiss, and I will let you go for the day."

She narrowed her eyes and kissed his lips, brushing her mouth against his and flicking her tongue against him. He held her tight to him and slid his thigh between hers. He pressed it firmly against the juncture of her thighs while he rocked her hips against him.

She gasped, and his tongue started to thrust and retreat as he gripped her hips and moved her against him. Her body took up the beat, and she flexed her hips on him, her clit enjoyed the friction and pressure, and she felt the rush of heat a moment before she shivered and bucked against him.

He continued the slow grind of her hips against his thigh, and she twitched and shuddered with every aftershock.

He broke the kiss and leaned back, his dragon's eyes were smug. "Now you can go and have a good day."

She slammed her hand into his abdomen to stand up, and he grunted and didn't grab her again. She walked over to the drawer and found her passes. Without looking at him, she left the room, and when the door closed behind her, she exhaled slowly and fanned herself for a moment. Damp thighs were a small price to pay for waking up to that.

With a small smile, she headed for the entertainment center and got into her uniform. It was time to rescue the folks who tried to circumvent the scenarios.

Chapter Seven

$\mathcal{S}$ he was in her pod and finishing the extraction of a client who wanted to do whatever the hell he wanted in a group scenario. The other persons in his party did not appreciate his advances. He was pulled out by the back of his collar, and she threw him back into his body before filing her paperwork in her own pod.

"Styra." The voice in her pod was extremely familiar.

"Yes, Mr. Blue?"

He was amused as hell. "We have a non-compatible mind in pod sixteen. Can you get him out?"

"Sure. On my way."

She checked the scenario, found a

matching outfit for the situation, and sent herself in.

Her practical clothing had not made the transition. She was wearing the same fluttering and transparent silk that she had been wearing the last time she left this scenario. The heavy thudding of drake's wings was audible a moment before a huge clawed hand wrapped around her, flying her to the top of the tower.

She was set down gently, and the back of his clawed knuckle stroked down her spine. She reached up and stroked his chin, pressing a soft kiss to the side of his scaled head. "Hello again."

He shivered, and his wings flexed.

She ran her hand along the rough surface of his nose and jaw. He closed his eyes and let out a low rumble before he huffed and pushed her toward the bed.

She smiled and walked toward the bed where it seemed that as unlikely as it was,

Yr-el had fallen into the same trap.

She stood next to him and watched the stars moving under his skin. She traced her fingers across a falling star and followed it to his navel and beneath to the edge of the skirt he was wearing.

Styra moved over him and straddled one of his legs while she slowly leaned toward his lips. She glanced at the drake, and he was watching intently. She winked at him, and she licked at Yr-el's lips.

"I suppose that this requires some planning. It can't be too short, and it would be a shame if it was too long." She leaned in and kissed him again, flicking her tongue along his lips before lifting her head just short of the time limit.

"Well, that didn't work." She plastered herself on top of him and kissed him, holding onto his head until he shifted under her. He stroked his hands over her back, up and then down again. He slid his hands into the openings on the sides of her dress and cupped her butt, pulling her against him.

He kept his eyes closed, and she lifted her head. "Hmm. Looks like you aren't awake yet. Whatever am I to do?"

Without opening his eyes, he leaned up and kissed her, his tongue twisting against hers as his hips undulated under her. She felt herself getting slick, and he held her tight, flipping her to her back before leaning back with his eyes glowing and his smile focused.

"Look at that. You managed to wake me."

He tugged at the ties holding her dress up, and they snapped, exposing her breasts with a deliberate bit of force. Yrel leaned down and kissed and sucked at her breasts in turn. She heard the small sounds coming from her throat and lifted her hips against him. She flinched when her body tensed, and he smiled against her skin and gripped her hands, pulling them up and pinning them above her head. He dragged his hand up her inner thigh and slid a finger inside her before inserting a second. He groaned against her breasts. "Stars, you are wet."

She shuddered, and he seemed to come to a decision. He pulled at his waistband, and the ornate skirt slithered away. His erection made her widen her eyes. It wasn't the size; it was the slow and deliberate twist that it was executing.

He snagged the top of her dress and split it down the center with the crook of his finger and a deliberate motion. It distracted her while he slid onto her and his cock writhed against her.

His cock prodded and slowly slid into her. His gaze was silver, and he moved his hips in short and gentle jolts as he got further and further into her.

She locked eyes with him and lifted her legs to either side of his thighs as he slowly entered her. The fact that this was a scenario removed any aches or pains she was feeling.

Once he was in as far as she could take him, he began to move. Lights started to spin behind her lids as she tried to focus while she took up the rhythm with him. It was no use. Her analytical mind went out the window as she rocked and moved with him, gasping and moaning as her body suddenly started to shake and twitch. He thrust into her quickly and groaned, shuddering as he took his weight on his elbows.

Yr-el remained inside her, and he slowly looked up, smiling at her. "So, how long can we stay in here before Mbrak pulls the plug?"

"Two hours forty-six minutes." Her projected form was catching its breath. She felt a random aftershock grip him, and he blinked.

There was a distinct stirring inside

her, and she felt the slow twisting and plunging while the rest of Yr-el remained stationary.

She shivered and clutched his sides. "Two forty-five."

He grinned and kissed her. They had time to kill.

Mbrak saw the strange readings from Styra's suit. He chuckled and summoned his current feed manager.

Abil came in. "What is it, boss?"

He sighed. "I keep telling you it is either grandfather or Mr. Blue."

"Yes, boss."

"There is going to be a new imperial service commander coming in tomorrow. I want you to make sure that the hotel is ready and that Styra is not to cross his path."

"Sure, boss, but why? Styra does most of the meet and greets."

"She is in heat and will be occupied with her new mate. It took me long enough to find the bastard; I am not letting him leave until she has what she needs."

"She's . . . right. Okay. That explains a bit." Abil smiled and made a note. She liked her notes. They kept everything moving along.

"Had you noticed?"

"She has smelled a little floral for the last few days. I know she doesn't use perfume, so it makes sense that she is going through a little something weird. When will she be back to normal duties?"

Mbrak smiled. "I think she will be leaving us soon."

"Why?"

Mbrak turned to his second-eldest granddaughter. "When you meet your mate, you will know it. Distance is not an option. You have to be with him for a few years, at the very least."

"Oh. So, why would she go with him, boss?"

"She has no choice. If she's in heat, her drake is waking up, and he is encouraging it."

"Whoa. She has a drake? Why hasn't she shown it off?" Abil's voice was vapid, but Mbrak knew she worked hard at it. She was keenly intelligent, but it made her life easier to pretend to be clueless.

"It isn't awake yet. It would be extremely dangerous if it woke up on the station, so I am trying to get the good captain to take our Styra with him when he returns home."

"Why would he leave her if he knows she is his mate?"

Mbrak chuckled. "Things are complicated. They will work it out."

Abil asked, "Boss, what if they don't?"

He grinned. "Her drake wakes and kills us all."

"Oh. Shit. I am hoping they work it out

then."

Mbrak laughed and turned back to his screens.

Styra woke in her chair with a gasp and answered the com request. "Styra, head to your quarters. You are having erratic life signs. Get some rest."

She looked around. "I am fine."

She was fine. Her knees were weak, her pulse was rapid, and her crotch was soaked, but she was fine.

Mr. Blue's voice came through the speaker. "Take. The. Day. Off."

She sighed. "Fine. I will take the day off."

Styra headed for the change room and smiled at Abil.

Her friend smiled. "Heading out?"

"Yeah. Apparently, my stats were all over the place."

Abil chuckled. "I looked up drakes in

heat, and I think you should relax."

Styra paused. "I am not in heat."

"Boss said you were. He's a drake. He would know."

Styra blinked. "I . . . I don't know. I don't think I am."

Abil patted her on the shoulder. "Take a day to unwind anyway. You work too hard."

"Thanks." Styra went to change and hung her sensor suit in the cleaning unit. The suit from the dispenser was hanging in her locker, but Styra had a change of clothing of the exercise vein. She thought about working out and smiled. That was just what she was up for.

She was setting up one of the lift machines when she noticed that Yr-el's men were nearby. They hadn't seen her, or she certainly wouldn't have overheard one of them saying, "As soon as we finish delivering the captain to the woman his parents have picked out, we can relax."

Styra froze in place for a moment, and then, she settled herself in the machine to begin doing a press. His family had chosen a bride for him. Of course, they had. She was a stupid, damaged nobody from the middle of the star system. Why would she end up with him? Another two days and he would be gone.

She used both arms on the press for the first time in her adult life, and when she had done a set of five, it increased the weight. She kept going.

Yr-el looked at Mbrak. "What do you want? I was going to try and find Styra."

Mbrak looked him over. "Is she yours?"

"Of course, she is. My parents are going to show off another fine lady, but it is Styra who is my mate. He won't accept anything else."

"Good. She kicked into heat with a vengeance this morning, and she will need to be removed from the station sooner rather than later."

Yr-el felt his skin heat. "She's in heat?"

"Yeah, it fired into full bloom while she was on shift. You wouldn't know anything about that, now, would you?"

Yr-el shrugged. "Your guess is as good as mine."

A beep got their attention, and Mbrak answered. "What?"

"Um, sir? There is an incident occurring in the gym. Weight section."

Mbrak brought the displays up, and there was Styra, glowing white-hot with a grimace on her face. The unit she was working in displayed her pressing over one thousand kilos.

"She's waking." Mbrak's voice was flat.

Yr-el spoke quickly. "Where is the nearest emergency hatch?"

Mbrak brought the map up and

showed him.

"Tell them I am on my way."

"Watch out, Yr-el, she looks mad. I will evacuate your path."

Yr-el was on his way to the gym, wondering what the hell had set her off.

She stepped out of the machine when Yr-el came toward her. "You have a fiancé. Your parents have chosen your mate."

He slowed down, and he looked worried. "They have chosen a dozen so far. I reject them all."

She could see her skin glowing brightly, and she shivered. "They said that your parents had your woman."

He winced. "A woman. Not mine. You are mine. You are coming home with me."

She felt the white-hot rage subside, but something else was taking its place. "I don't know what is going on."

He nodded. "I know. Let me carry you. We need to get out of here."

She nodded and held out her arms like a child. He grabbed her, swung her into his arms, and he sprouted wings that scooped the air and propelled them through the station. He pulled her to the emergency airlock and stepped into the space between the chambers.

"Do you trust me, Styra?" He looked at her earnestly.

"I do. I am getting hotter."

He nodded. "I know. Just remember that the stars are where you get what you need. Turn toward them and take it in."

She didn't know what he meant, but he hit the outer door lock, and it slowly cycled open. The heat in her body ratcheted up a notch, and she saw her skin blurring.

When the door opened, they were sucked out, and he shifted into the drake that she knew from the scenario. Space should have begun killing her. She should have frozen or boiled, or whatever space farers whispered about late at night. Instead, she was caught in a claw and flown away from the station.

She relaxed and watched ships and chunks of rock go past as Yr-el took her toward the nearest star. The heat in her body increased, and he threw her away from him. She saw him as she tumbled away, but then, her body was busy becoming a drake.

She curled up in a ball, and then, she extended outward, flexing her wings and flicking her tail. She was still tumbling. A tail wrapped around hers, controlling her spiral. She locked claws with him, and her wings began to help her control the radiation that she was putting out.

Once her rotation was under control, she looked to Yr-el, and she pushed off, flapping her wings and flying through the depths of space.

Yr-el watched the bright burn of power that she exuded in a heavy blast at the moment of transformation. The blast of radiation would have killed any humans or similar species nearby. He had gotten her as far away from the station as he could before she began to burn his claw.

He was stunned when she transformed. She was graceful and elegant, moonlight come alive. He moved to stop her rotation by grabbing her tail and following it up with his rear claws. He was so very careful until she shoved him away, and then, the chase was on.

Her drake moved easily for a new transformation, and she caught on to charging herself with the light of the nearest star. The wide panels of her wings were nearly translucent, but power coursed below the skin. She was fantastic—light, power, and grace with glowing blue eyes.

He watched her play and then was amused when she began a game of tag with him. She nudged him and flew away, looking over her shoulder at him. She was flirting.

His dragon rose to the occasion and chased his mate. They flew around the safe zone where she had shifted, but gradually, she began to slow. It was time for her to return to the station, but he wasn't sure how to get her there.

She suddenly looked at him and then turned herself toward Blue Station. She got a good bit of speed under her wings, and then, she glided back toward the shuttle dock. He knew where she was aiming but wasn't sure as to her ability to shift on command.

He kept at her side, protecting her from incoming aircraft. The exterior door opened, and the magnetic door was all that was left between them and their landing. Unfortunately, neither of them would fit.

She was giggling as she sped up and powered toward the shuttle bay. Styra focused on the shape she wanted and when she wanted to change, and as she hit the magnetic shield, she changed into her human shape again and slid to a skidding stop on the floor of the hangar.

Yr-el landed behind her, fully dressed and with his wings. She flipped to her side with her knee drawn up. He was panting and glaring down at her.

She looked up at him and asked calmly, "So, no fiancé?"

He growled and picked her up, tossing her naked butt skyward and over his shoulder as he walked out of the shuttle bay and through the station. She was too tired to put up much of a fight . . . for now.

Chapter Eight

Styra blinked as she was flipped from his shoulder and onto the bed in his hotel room. The entire station between the shuttle bay and the hotel had been treated to the view of her backside.

He pinned her between his hands and loomed over her.

She looked him up and down. "Why do you get to shift with clothing, and mine exploded?"

He paused and sighed, shuddering, and his clothing simply vanished. "Practice."

He kissed her, and she pressed her hands to his shoulders; he pinned her arms above her head and began to work his way down her body with lips and tongue.

She was shocked for a few seconds, and then, she held her breath as she anticipated where he would touch next. She jumped when he parted her thighs and lifted his head. His left hand was holding her wrists together, and his right hand worked between her thighs.

When he slid his fingers into her, he shuddered. He withdrew his hand and released her wrists, kneeling on the bed and pulling her hips up along his thighs. He fitted his cock to her and pulled her hips against him with a hard pull.

She gasped and hissed at the sudden burn of him inside her. It didn't hurt, but it wasn't comfortable.

He slid a hand under her back and pulled her into his lap, still embedded inside her. She shuddered and held onto him as his cock started moving inside her. She slid her hands around his neck and pulled his head to hers, kissing him as he began the first of several couplings that took them hours to complete.

Styra faded in and out after the fourth or fifth round, and she had lost count of how many times her body had shaken and clutched at him. She was lying face down with him still inside her, covered in sweat and shivering as her body randomly twitched.

He was pressed against her back, still inside her, his arm next to hers.

She tried to focus and asked him blearily, "Did you just lick me pretty much everywhere?"

He chuckled. "It is a drake grooming behaviour."

She grumbled. "I am pretty sure that the drakes don't pin their partner's arms behind their back to complete the grooming."

"I improvised." He pressed a kiss to one of half a dozen marks he had left on her shoulders.

"So. I have another form."

"That is the conclusion that has been drawn. You are beautiful, by the way. Living moonlight."

"Um, thank you. You are rather striking in that form yourself." She sighed, "What happens next?"

"I head back to my family's domain. You come with me. We settle into the new normal from there. Mbrak has already given his full authorization for you to leave the station."

"Of course, he did. I am sure that he lured you here the moment he thought something was going on with me."

"He did not lure me, he invited me. As he is the elder in charge of this region, I was obligated to visit when he requested that we swing through. I am very glad that the imperial house was amenable to the request."

He was warm, so warm while they had

this conversation, his mouth idly nibbling at her shoulder. He murmured, "So, your drake was waiting for healing."

The words out of his mouth caused her appetite to roar to life. Her stomach growled angrily.

She groaned. "I am sweaty, sticky, stuck, and now hungry. This is not what I had planned for today."

"Physical sex is a lot messier than it is in a scenario, well, at least if you do it right." He chuckled. "I will order food, help you bathe, and hopefully, the bots will have managed to find all the sheets and tidy up the bed."

She moved sluggishly and winced. Her body was limp, and the smallest movement took tremendous effort. Yr-el pulled out of her and moved around the room while she tried to unsuccessfully push herself upright. She got halfway up, saw the wreck of bed, fixtures, and sweaty body prints on the walls. She flexed her shoulders. *Oh. Right.*

Yr-el was going to have a helluva cleaning bill. Maybe she could extend him her discount.

He sent the catering request and walked over to her, looking obnoxiously spry and alert.

"Come on. The first shift hurts the worst. Your body has been compressed, and it isn't fond of the feeling."

He lifted her and carried her to the bathroom, sitting her on the small chair near the shower wand before rinsing her skin of obvious traces of their mating.

She looked at him with squinted eyes. "Oh. Yes. I am sure it is just the transformation that is causing aches and pains. Nothing else of note has occurred."

He grinned but kept working on her until she was shivering but ready for a bath. The bath was full, and he helped her into it before quickly rinsing himself off and then joining her. He pulled her toward him and settled her with her back to his chest.

"Is this so that I don't bite you?" She grumbled.

He chuckled. "That might be a concern. It certainly helps when I am inside you. Your little jaws pack a powerful amount of compression."

Styra snorted and turned slightly, seeing the bite mark on his neck. "Yeah, that was fun."

He snorted and slowly moved his hands over her. Caressing rather than arousing. It was like he was petting her.

"So, tomorrow, we will leave for my home. Do you have any objections?"

She sighed. "Can my cousins visit?"

"Cousins?"

"There are close to a dozen of us here. All related to Mr. Blue, a bunch of generations back and all about to step foot into being drakes ourselves. He's been matchmaking for generations." She watched as he placed her hand between his and made a strange sandwich.

"That is interesting. I will have to ask my father about it. I mean, I know some drakes go out and create progeny without finding a mate, but it isn't recommended. Their partners don't always survive."

She chuckled. "Mr. Blue's partners all survived. He took care of them, but I still have no idea why the elders would send one of their own out for this purpose?"

"The universe is expanding. Colonies are being formed in every habitable corner of every star system. We are needed." He pressed his lips to her shoulder.

"So, I am in heat?"

He chuckled against her skin. "Yes. Definitely."

She nodded. "How long will it last?"

"Don't know. A day, a week, a month? No idea. I will be here for you."

He bit her shoulder gently, and she shivered. "Oh. Great. That has a tone of cheerful menace to it."

He chuckled against her skin. "Good. You are paying attention."

He licked her shoulder and neck before turning her with a splash and pulling her astride him. The moment that his cock found her opening, she thrust her hips and took him inside her with the water sloshing around them. She slowly rode him, his hands stroking her breasts and cupping her hips, sliding over her and pulling her in so he could use his mouth on her skin. The friction caused by the water rinsing away her essence was sweet, and it was heightened by the nipping kisses that Yr-el gave her while she slowly rode him until she arched back and shuddered in his arms.

The message on the flashing com was from Mr. Blue, and they listed as they ate. *Styra, you are hereby relieved of duty and are assigned to the Ackerwol*

Imperium. Your base will be Harva. Your position is as security protocol programmer. Your cousins want to throw you a going-away party if your mate will part with you for a few hours.

She blinked. "Harva? Where the hell is Harva?"

He chuckled. "It is my home. We have two dozen large cities and lots of open space. It is the ideal place to raise offspring."

She froze. "Offspring?"

"Certainly. That is what your heat is about. I am surprised that Mbrak is encouraging you to meet up with your relatives."

She curled up, and he wrapped around her back. "What is so weird about me meeting up with my cousins?"

"Well, unless I miss my guess, they are all female, and as you are in a strong heat, you will begin the process to trigger the ones who are developed enough to pursue a mate of their own." He slid his hand down and pressed it to her belly. "That is if your heat is still active."

Her body had lit up when he ran his hand across her skin, but she sighed. "I don't give a fuck what my body wants right now. My brain needs sleep."

He chuckled. "Then, as long as I can touch you, sleep it shall be."

She gave a low huff and wiggled against him to get comfortable and make him uncomfortable. She wished that she had been able to keep the smirk off her face. He stroked a hand across her cheek and turned her head for a kiss. Her body warmed rapidly, and then, he cuddled her close, chuckling softly.

She closed her eyes and pretended that the slight contact hadn't set her blood on fire.

Her body was content to rest, but she was not going to sleep deeply. She had an agenda to plan for. When she was dumped on a new world, she was going to need a plan and possibly some clothing that didn't have a magnetic closure.

Dancing for hours with her cousins was highly enjoyable. Mr. Blue had given them all a few hours off and was managing the entertainment center himself during that time.

Styra enjoyed flinging her limbs around with her cousins, but it was disconcerting that Yr-el had invited himself to the party. Weirdly, the ladies had been happy to have him.

Styra was still aching from her previous activity, so she took a seat in the private room of the club near the port. Abil was there, smiling with her clipboard in her hands.

"You look happy, Styra." Abil nodded as if affirming her identification of the emotion she was seeing.

Styra sipped at a juice. "I am. I think. I

don't know. It has been so long since I felt more than the small trill of excitement when rescuing a client. Now, it seems to happen every few minutes when I am with him."

"Really? Exciting?" Abil frowned. "Maybe I should get my own. I am next eldest, after all."

Styra chuckled. "You won't have to look too hard. I think that now that we are all adults, Mr. Blue has decided to bring the mates to us. Mine was just the first."

Abil chuckled. "There is another one on the way right now. His ship is docking right now, but I am to keep you away from him. Your pheromones are a little potent."

Styra blinked. "Really? I can't smell them."

"You smell like sweet flowers to me, but the boss said that you would smell different to each drake."

118

"He mentioned this to you?"

"Yeah, he seemed concerned about you but amused and cheerful at the same time."

Styra glanced at the corner where Yr-el was sitting. He was leaning back casually, and he had a drink in one hand. Even from across the room, she could see the stars moving under his skin.

There was a stack of parcels for her, and each had a new outfit that didn't look like something that would suit her for daily work but, instead, looked very pretty and feminine. Abil smiled. "Mr. Blue's suggestion, as well. He said that you wouldn't need bodysuits and that your mate would appreciate skirts for your daily wear."

Styra hugged her. "Thank you."

"So, he healed you, huh? That's good." Abil reiterated what the other girls had first exclaimed at.

"It hurt like hell, but it has helped me

119

to move like an average person. No more hunching over in pain. Getting used to food is strange, but that will probably come with time."

Abil nodded. "I can see that it would be a problem. The supplements that you had to take were far more extensive than the ones we take."

Styra paused. "You are on supplements as well? You never said."

"We all are. I am guessing it is a top-up of the boss's blood, but we all take it, and it helps us with the interface." Abil smiled. "Your mate's ship will be leaving tomorrow morning. There isn't a gate window, but he says that you need to go."

Styra blinked. "So, that is the reason for the emergency party. I had better hug my way out of here. I am so tired."

Abil nodded. "The first shift and an entire day of coitus would take it out of you. Be well, and I would like to visit you if I am able."

"I would like that." It would be a touch of something familiar to have her cousins visit one by one.

Abil nodded again. "I will have your new clothing brought to the captain's ship." She made notes on her clipboard and smiled brightly.

"Thank you, Abil. You always know what needs to be done." Styra smiled. "Despite your slow start, you have the quickest wit that I have ever dealt with."

"I wish I could speak as fast as I think, but that is what I have to work with. I do get a little better each day." Abil sighed.

Styra hugged her again. Her cousin had arrived unable to speak at the age of ten. She had been found in a forest, living alone, and Mr. Blue had arranged for her delivery to the station. Like the rest of his descendants, she had ended up alone. It was a curse that had touched most of those related to Mbrak the Blue.

She looked around the group and

sighed. Every one of them was orphans through death or surrender.

Styra got up, hugged her way through her relatives, and then, she went over to Yr-el, and she crawled into his lap. She sighed deeply.

"Are you all right?"

She nodded. "I am. I am exhausted, and I will miss them all in my own particular way."

"Have you been drinking?"

"Only juice. I have no idea what kind of reaction I would have if I imbibed." She sighed. "My organs are still settling in."

He kissed the top of her head. "It is best to take some things slowly."

She grinned and looked up at him. "That isn't what you said right before the party."

"That was different." He smiled and kissed her. "That was for mutual gratification."

She sighed. "So, we leave tomorrow, huh?"

"How did you . . ."

"Abil. She talks slow, but she knows everything. She's the true second-in-command on this station."

He nodded. "I am beginning to understand the role that you and your relations play on this station. I got a copy of your resume when you were getting dressed. You can really code that quickly?"

She nodded. "That was my skill. I can react rapidly to the information flow, and I can bend it just enough to slip past."

She paused and then said, "I am ready to leave if you are."

He grinned. "Sweeter words have never reached my ears."

He picked her up, and her relatives cheered her as she was carried off to the hotel for a good night's rest.

She laughed for five minutes at the thought that she was going to get much sleep.

Chapter Nine

She held still as the ship disconnected from the station and floated away. The crew was seated at the controls, and Yr-el had left her with a quick kiss to the cheek and retreated to another part of the ship.

"Where did he go?" She asked the crew.

The lieutenant chuckled. "He is going to fly out, grab the ship in his mouth, and then tear a hole in space to get us directly to Harva. No delays." There were a pause and an alarm. "There he goes."

She looked at the monitor and saw the drake circling the ship before they jolted, and they started moving forward at an accelerated pace. He moved them around the traffic approaching the station with ease, and her heart thudded as she left her home.

The ship rocked and rattled as Yr-el picked up speed. Styra gripped the sides of her seat, and she winced. "Save the rough ride for solid ground, Yr-el."

The rocking immediately smoothed out, and the ship hurtled toward a rift that appeared in front of them. There was a low hum of a growl that went through the entire ship in response to her words.

She looked at the speed and the smoothness of the vessel's trajectory. "Can he hear me?"

The crew was laughing at her, and she blushed. She may or may not have propositioned her mate. Her body was still humming from his early morning attention.

They shot through the rift and came out the other side in a matter of minutes.

Harva was waiting for them, a bright and lively world.

Yr-el carried them to a point near one of the moons and released the ship for landing.

They descended, and he followed them to the port on the surface. Styra watched the progress, and she found it fascinating that they could travel so quickly from world to world with a drake controlling them.

When they were settled, the lieutenant stood next to her. "We are offloading your things to Yr-el's home. He will probably want to fly you there as soon as you clear customs."

"Customs?"

He nodded. "Just like on the station. Certain worlds require registry of transient populations. You won't have any trouble."

Styra rubbed her hands on her skirt and stood up. The gravity felt weird.

127

She was escorted out of the ship and to customs by his men. With the guard of the imperium next to her, she was eased past the crowds and then faced customs. The sneer on the face of the inspector was obvious.

Styra faced him and extended her travel documentation.

"I see you are from Blue Station."

"Yes."

"The pleasure station."

She cocked her head. "Entertainment. Yes."

"So, are you planning on charging for your services here?" His brows were drawn together.

"Of course. No one works for free." She could see the denial in his expression before he said anything. "I have received my transfer documents as a security specialist for Harva."

He paused. "What?"

"Second from the bottom. Imperium

staffing transfer."

He flipped through, and he paused. "This says that you have commander ranking."

She smiled. "I suppose it does."

He scowled. "Please, place your hand on the screen and identify your species."

She put her hand on the screen and grinned. "Drake."

He froze. "Pardon me?"

"Drake. I am a drake. Run all the scans you like, it will still be the same result."

His sneer was back. "If you are a drake, why didn't you land outside the port?"

"Well, in the first place, I don't like to do things illegally; in the second, I am also very new and have only changed form once. I don't want to make things awkward as I settle in."

"Settle in? Have you seduced one of the crew of the warship you came in on?"

The door to the interview room opened, and Yr-el growled. "Why is she in

here, Rabor? You know better than to de-
tain a drake in heat."

The inspector shot to his feet and
bowed. "Master Yr-el. I am so sorry. I
didn't know she was yours."

Styra smiled. "We were getting there.
He was fixated on sex, but I think we
were getting around to why I was sent
here."

Yr-el pulled her to her feet. "Give me
her documents."

The inspector scrambled and put the
stack together before handing it over. "I
apologize, miss. You should have stated
your relationship the moment that you
entered."

"I thought it would sound tacky." She
looked up at Yr-el.

He wrapped his arms around her and
kissed her, pulling her against him and
lifting her until they were face to face. She
draped her arms around his neck, and
when he lifted his head, he whispered,

"Look at him."

She turned her head, and the inspector looked terrified. "Do I have clearance to enter?"

He nodded and bent over to type swiftly. "You have clearance, Styra Il-Mbrak. Welcome to Harva."

Yr-el grinned. "Excellent. She does try and do things technically correct. When she wasn't out immediately, I knew that she hadn't given all of the necessary information upon entering your office. Thank you, Rabor. Good day."

He carried her out of the office, away from customs, and down the hall. His wings were still present as he walked out of the building and took flight.

She held onto his neck as he flew swiftly over the nearby city and headed toward the countryside. She had never seen that many trees and green spaces outside of a scenario.

She pulled herself up so she could

whisper in his ear. "Where are we going?"

"My family home."

"Why?"

He chuckled. "That is where we are going to live. We are nearly there. Look."

She turned her head and gasped. Perched on a tall cliff was a castle that was very similar to the one in the scenario he preferred.

"It's the castle."

He chuckled. "Almost. When I saw it in the catalogue, I knew it was the one for me. I hadn't read the fine print about the princess and the kiss, and I am very glad I didn't."

She smiled, and he landed with her, still stuck to him in the courtyard of the castle.

Smiling figures came out of the main entrance. A couple who looked to be five or ten years older than Styra and a young woman in an exquisite gown.

Yr-el kept his arm firmly around her as

he retracted his wings and walked toward the older couple. "Mother, Father, I am here to introduce my mate, Styra."

Styra was pulled along for the ride but left alone while his parents hugged him.

The young woman glared at her. "You? You are his mate? I very much doubt it."

Styra looked at her, and she heard the back of her dress tear. The other woman took a step back as Styra raised her wings and beat them twice, knocking the other woman on her ass. She folded her wings against her back and looked to Yr-el and his family. He was grinning proudly; his parents were standing with their jaws slightly open.

She bowed. "Please, allow me to introduce myself. I am Styra Il-Mbrak. Orphaned, taken in and raised by the blue drake of Blue Station."

His father stepped forward and bowed. "I am Ren-el, and this is my mate, Vanera."

"I am pleased to meet you. You have an exceptional son."

Yr-el snaked his arm around her waist. "And he has chosen an exceptional mate."

Styra looked at the young woman, and she was gone.

Ren-el winced. "Ah. The rumour was that you were faking a drake bride to throw off our attempts to find you a mate."

Styra dissipated her wings and stood with her hand pressed to her chest as the wings had torn the support out of her dress. She blushed. "The wings are new."

Vanera smiled. "But they are yours. I still haven't met mine yet. I am not old enough with enough drake material inside me."

Yr-el smiled. "Styra and her cousins are all fully drakes; they are just maturing."

Ren-el nodded. "That is what Mbrak

said. I didn't believe him, but he said if you took enough half-bloods over enough generations, the result would be a pure-blood with interesting characteristics."

She bowed. "I believe his words are accurate. I know my cousins. They are going to be fantastic drakes in the very near future."

Ren-el chuckled. "I don't know what the universe will do with an influx of female drakes."

Styra smiled brightly. "It will just have to suck it up."

Vanera laughed. "I like that attitude, but based on the look in Yr-el's eyes, you two need some privacy unless public displays are more up your alley of interest. Oh, and we are planning a ball to introduce you to the locals as soon as your heat is over."

She blushed. "You can tell?"

"Only from fifteen feet away." Vanera winked. "Don't worry. It happens to all of us."

Yr-el nodded and picked her up. "Well, we will see you in a few days. Send food."

Styra blushed but waved as she was flown up and over the castle into one of the spacious turret rooms.

Her heat was going to last as long as it lasted, and she was just going to have to get used to things around the castle and on Harva. It looked like the gravity here was the least of her worries. But, she could adapt, she would adapt, and she would stop radiating pheromones... eventually.

Ren-el exhaled softly. "That little lady is powerful. Her scent is enough to attract anyone within a radius of about two hundred meters."

"Really? I just thought she smelled like sweet flowers."

"No, she smells like sex, but Yr-el has

been working hard to keep his scent in the mix. I think we might end up with a grandchild or three." He chuckled.

Vanera looked toward her son's tower. "They grow up so fast."

"It has been fifty years. Perhaps we should try for another." He smiled slyly.

Vanera blinked. "Huh. I thought during your heat, you were trying like hell."

"I guess I should just try harder. Perhaps we should take a vacation. You know, let Yr-el take over with that little spot of moonlight at his side."

Vanera laughed. "I would not call her that to her face. She looks to have a bit of steel under the moonlight."

"Of course, she does. You haven't met Mbrak, but he is one of the coldest drakes I have ever met. He's stuck on that station for a good reason."

"What reason?"

"He killed one of his own. Our own. There aren't many of us, but those that

there are have an unspoken truce. He
tore another drake apart, and the station
was built as his prison. He was marked as
dangerous, and no mature drake is al-
lowed to go near him."

His wife hissed. "You let our son go
there?"

"Our son is not in his attack demo-
graphic." His expression cracked, and he
laughed. "Mbrak is fine."

"What?" She was giving him a dark
look.

"He was one of our peacekeepers who
was responsible for cataloguing the half-
blood children that a few drakes were
producing. One of them had no concern
for his partners and gave them nothing
extra to help them through the stressful
pregnancy. So, there was a pathway of orphans in Alkut's wake. Mbrak confronted
him, and they took to the stars to complete their battle. He did end up killing
Alkut, and his sentence was to live his life

to make sure that every one of Alkut's descendants was brought back into the
drake bloodlines. So, Mbrak set out to
have daughters while the station was being built, and he kept tabs on all of them,
every line. He sent out matchmakers
when the children were old enough, and
he connected their bloodlines, and then,
he did it again. The current generation is
the result of a lot of mixing and matching.
Each is descended from no less than four
drakes, and all of the girls are being
trained to have marketable skills. They
are very impressive via their resumes."

Vanera blinked. "What? You knew all
about her?"

Ren-el shrugged. "Of course. Mbrak
would not gain access to our son without
my agreement. It had been a while since
I had heard from him, and he is an elder,
so I listened when he spoke. We are now
guardians, by extension, to his Styra. I
just wanted to see them together before I

told you what was going on."

His mate was staring at him in shock. "What? Wait. Let me get this straight. You knew about her origins, about Mbrak's invitation to meet her, and the likelihood that she was going to be my son's mate, and you didn't tell me?"

Vanera' tone had gone calm and cold. Ren-el frowned. "Should I have told you before it happened? You don't like to be given all the options."

"Of course not. If I had had all the options, I wouldn't have ended up with you." She closed her mouth with a snap as he turned toward her.

He looked at his mate with narrowed eyes. "Hm. You are right. I think I should give you all of your options."

He grabbed her at the waist and flew upward, his head bent, and his lips pressed next to her ear, whispering all of the options that he would like to exercise if she was amenable. He didn't smile when she grabbed his head and kissed him, but he did turn back toward the castle that she had designed and he had constructed for her. The scent of a female in heat might not be having an effect that Vanera could sense, but he felt the change in his mate and grinned where she couldn't see him at the thought of another son with his mate's eyes.

Styra ran her hands down the skirt, and she looked at Yr-el. "Are you sure this looks okay?"

He sighed and kissed her hand. "It looks lovely, and you will be able to sprout your wings if you like to."

She looked at the soft, dark purple fabric that wrapped her breasts, was fastened behind her neck, and attached at the back of her skirt. The skirt was the same fabric, and the whole thing flowed and clung as she moved.

He held her hand as they walked into the ballroom, and silence fell. Panic hit her, and her wings sprouted, but he held her hand, and they walked down the steps. "You don't have to get away. No one here is going to hurt you."

"I know that, but I am not used to wearing this little outside of a scenario, and this is most definitely real." She managed to get her wings back under control and back into her body.

"You look lovely and like mine." He wagged his brows, and she snickered.

She squeezed his hand and smirked. "Yup. For as long as you last."

He paused, and then, he started laughing, and that is how they entered their reception. She was amused, he was laughing, and they were both entranced with each other while his parents made the introductions.

During dinner, Styra leaned over to

her mate and said, "There are folk glaring at me as if they wished I would burst into flames."

"Ah, they would be the family of the ladies who have been sent here to try and stumble into my bed. They belong to a variety of trade unions in the area."

She nodded. "Okay, that makes sense."

Vanera rose to her feet, and she smiled. "Thank you, one and all, for attending our little gathering here at Harva. Now that my son has managed to find and keep his mate, his father and are offering Yr-el and Styra one of our other worlds if they want to begin from nothing or this place if they want to remain here and take on our position of outpost guardians for the imperium."

Yr-el nodded. "We will remain here if you do not mind. Styra could use some stability around her."

The gathered group of nobles and

traders looked confused.

Ren-el smiled. "Well, now that the sun has set, we can go on to other things. The Blue Station has provided us and the imperium with some footage. It should stop the constant bids for your hand, son."

A projector flared to life over the ballroom, and everyone looked up. The exterior was Blue Station, and a dark and a glowing object emerged from one of the airlocks. The dark object grew, and in a flash, Yr-el the drake was grabbing the smaller glowing item in his claw and flying away from the station.

The projection was taken up by another satellite, and the ball of light went right past the camera before the drake followed and stayed at a safe distance.

Yr-el took Styra's hand, and she watched the moment of her first transformation. She formed a tight ball and then stretched out, her body absorbing the small rocks and debris that were in her expansion zone.

After that, she started to play tag with him.

She turned toward Yr-el, and he kissed her. "It was a very good first shift, Styra. You should be pleased with it."

"I am. I just forgot that the area is lined with monitors and video devices. It wasn't at the forefront in my mind at the time."

He grinned. "This moment is being broadcast to every elder with any kind of descendants who are capable of a shift. They will be begging Mbrak for an introduction, but if they are wise, they will simply send their best."

She chuckled. "Is that your classification?"

His eyes were bright. "I am an opportunist. Just lucky to be close enough to Blue Station when he called. I figured it was worth an introduction; I just wasn't expecting to be exploited by a computer glitch."

She smiled. "And I wasn't expecting to have to kiss you and then you again to wake you, but it seems to have worked out."

"I needed you, you needed healing, and now, I wake you up with kisses. It has all come full circle." He kissed her hand and then stroked her cheek and started a kiss that had some of the humans around them giving off scents of heat.

Styra whispered, "Is that what I smell like?"

His eyes widened, and he laughed, "No, you smell like peaches and roses. The stronger the scent, the deeper you are in your heat."

"Ah. They smell like sweat and musk."

He grinned. "Yeah, they do."

Styra nodded. "Okay, sense of smell is kicking in. Huh. Who knew that that would come after the full shift and wings?"

He laughed and hugged her. "The order of things that you are involved in is peculiar, but that seems to be the way that you go through life. I now stand forewarned."

She smiled. He smiled, and the party got going.

Yorath the Gold was sitting on his throne when the projection of the newly mated pair completed. "How many of these cobbled-together dragons did Mbrak have?"

His assistant bowed. "Close to two dozen, Your Imperial Highness. The exact number is unsure. He will not respond to our queries."

Yorath looked at his assistant, and he snorted. "You tried to ask for one?"

"I thought it would be a good idea to bring them here and let you pick one as mate, Your Imperial Highness."

Yorath smiled. "It does not work that

way. I will send a note to Mbrak, and if he has a suitable descendant for me, he will let me know. It is a good thing, in general, though. I am very pleased with the new arrivals. Human body-born drakes are less powerful, but they are faster, so we shall see what becomes of him and his station." There was time. That was the one thing that Yorath had in abundance. If one of the new couples had daughters, that would work out as well. There was plenty of time, and suddenly, many more drakes were on the horizon.

He smiled. He did love moments of change in history, and he was watching one.

Author's Note

Well, this could have started off a new series . . . and it might do it one day. For now . . . the drakes will keep appearing when I need them.

Thanks for having patience with my weird journey through an unfocused mind, e.g., the Stand-Alone Tales. They have been fun and very calming for me.

Just a few more to get out of my head. Probably. Maybe. Perhaps.

Thanks for reading,

Viola Grace

About the Author

Viola Grace (aka Zenina Masters) is a Canadian sci-fi/paranormal romance writer with ambitions to keep writing for the rest of her life. She specializes in short stories because the thrill of discovery, of all those firsts, is what keeps her writing.

An artist who enjoys a story that catches you up, whirls you around, and sets you down with a smile on your face is all she endeavours to be. She prefers to leave the drama to those who are better suited to it, she always goes for the cheap laugh.

In real life, she is now engaged in bee-keeping, and her adventures can be found on the YouTube channel, Mystery Bees Apiary. Just look for the cartoon kittens.

Made in United States
Orlando, FL
08 August 2023

35892200R00085